MW00948560

An Awesome Christmas Gift

By: Dr. Madonna Taylor Higgs

Dedication

I can do all things through Christ who strengthens me.
Philippians 4:13

For: Terran, Nalau, TJ, Terrell, mom, dad, brothers, sisters, nieces, nephews, family, and friends!

Thank you, Lord, for guiding me!

“Look at all these presents! I have three, and they’re all pink, my favorite color!” exclaimed Nia.

"I have three presents too!" shouted Sam. "I can't wait to see what Santa brought me this year. Only seven more days to go!"

"You only have one gift." Nia snickered, glancing at SJ, who was standing in the doorway. "I'm glad I'm not the eldest."

“I don’t mind not getting a lot of gifts,” SJ said, smiling. “I have an AWESOME gift!”

“Awesome?” Sam clapped gleefully. “Where? How? I want one!” he whined.

"An awesome gift," Nia said, nodding her head. "Now, I can get with that!" I would have the best toys."

"I want some toys too, Nia. You can't have everything," said Sam.

“The gift I’m talking about is better than any of these things,” SJ said, gesturing around the room.

“Better than dolls and trucks! How?” Nia and Sam screamed.

"Sit down, and I will tell you," said SJ. "It all began with the very first gift."

"The reason we call December 25 Christmas," said SJ.

"Huh? Christmas? The reason why?" asked Sam.

"You're not making sense, SJ," Nia huffed, folding her arms. "Stop playing with us! I'm telling Mom." She rolled her eyes.

“Nia, just sit back and listen,” SJ said calmly. “I will tell you the story of the first Christmas. It all began with a girl named Mary.”

"This happened a long, long time ago," SJ explained. "Mary lived in a town called Nazareth. She was engaged to a man named Joseph."

“Marriage!” interrupted Nia. “Aww! I bet the wedding was beautiful.”

“Shh, Nia,” Sam growled.

SJ continued, "One day, while Mary was at home, an angel from God appeared and told her she was highly favored. She was chosen to have a baby boy, who she would name Jesus."

"Wait! I thought Mary was engaged. She was going to have a baby?" Sam asked.

Nia giggled. "Joseph must have been mad."

SJ nodded. "He was disappointed and was going to break up with her. But an angel appeared to Joseph and told him to marry Mary, so he did."

“Mary and Joseph got married and had to go out of town,” said SJ.

HOTEL
NO ROOMS

“Then Mary went into labor. It was time for the baby to be born. All the hotel rooms in the city of Bethlehem were full, so they had to go to a barn.”

“Wait a minute!” Nia shouted. “I thought you said this baby was King of the world! He was born in a barn? That doesn’t sound right!”

“Yes, Nia. He is the King of the world and was born in a barn,” SJ replied.

“Nearby, shepherds tended their flocks. An angel appeared and told them about the birth of Jesus Christ, the Savior,” SJ continued. “The shepherds set out in search of Christ.”

"Wise men from different countries traveled to see Jesus and celebrate his birth. A star led them to the King, Jesus Christ, who was resting in a manger."

"The wise men presented Christ with gifts of gold, frankincense, and myrrh," said SJ.

“So we get gifts because it’s Jesus’s birthday?” said Sam, clasping his hands.

“I can’t believe the men traveled so far to bring the baby gifts! He must be the King!” exclaimed Nia.

"That was the first time gifts were given to celebrate the birth of Jesus, the Christ in Christmas!" said SJ.

"At Christmas, we celebrate God's gift to us, and that gift is Jesus Christ!" SJ declared.

Sam and Nia grinned. "The first Christmas gift really was the greatest of all!" they shouted.

CPSIA information can be obtained
at www.ICGtesting.com
Printed in the USA
BVHW060003300921
617775BV00002B/166

9 781087 890586